Check out these other exciting
▼ STECK-VAUGHN Adventures

Get ready for a bumpy ride! Travel on
SNAKE RIVER

Where there's smoke. . . there's fire
Read all about it in
SMOKE

Is   e's poem?

                     E

ugh to rough it?
Check out the boys who
DON'T LOOK BACK

They're burning rubber in the desert heat!
See who in
ROAD RALLY

Is the big prize worth a big risk?
Get the answer in
VIDEO QUEST

Danger lies where eagles soar. Find out why in
SOARING SUMMER

The chase is on — but who's hunting who?
Find out, read
DANGEROUS GAME

A family can survive anything, right?
Learn more in
SNOW TREK

Produced by Mega-Books of New York, Inc.
Design and Art Direction by Michaelis/Carpelis Design Assoc.

Cover illustration: Ken Spencer

KNIGHT MOVES

by Pam Cardiff

interior illustrations by
Marcy Ramsey

STECK-VAUGHN
COMPANY

CHAPTER 1

"Go, Dawn! Go!" shouted Marilyn Kaba. Marilyn watched from the bleachers as her best friend Dawn Philips sprinted by. Dawn was practicing with the Millbrook High track team. She was the team's star runner and one of Millbrook's best all-around athletes. Marilyn could just picture her friend at the Olympics someday. She imagined Dawn's long legs and arms pumping hard as she triumphantly crossed the finish line.

"It's a bird! It's a plane! It's Dawn Philips, the fastest feet in the East!" Marilyn's daydream was broken as Joey

Coletta plopped down on the bleachers beside her. His blond hair stuck up like a bristly brush, and he was wearing his usual goofy grin. Marilyn sighed. Joey's class-clown act could be so annoying. But he was a nice guy, and a good friend of Dawn's.

"Dawn is looking good," said Marilyn. "We'll definitely beat Westwood High in the hurdles and 100-yard dash this Saturday."

"We'll destroy them!" Joey proclaimed.

Marilyn had to smile. Joey wasn't much of an athlete himself, but he sure was generous on team spirit.

Marilyn and Joey watched the runners for a while. Then Marilyn turned to Joey. "Did you hear that Medieval Days is coming up at the end of the month? It's a cool idea, don't you think? A whole day of tournaments just like in the days of the knights. It will give our school another chance to demolish Westwood."

"Yeah, it will be cool, all right," Joey agreed. "Entertaining, too. I've signed up to play the court jester."

"Do you think you can handle it?" asked Marilyn, grinning. "Jesters are supposed to be funny."

"Then I'll just hold up a picture of you," teased Joey. "That should be good for laughs."

Marilyn ignored his remark. She

turned her attention back to Dawn, who was now flying over the hurdles.

"You know," said Joey, "it's a drag that Dawn can't compete in Medieval Days. I bet she'd make a pretty good knight."

"What do you mean, Dawn can't compete?" asked Marilyn. "She'd make a great knight!"

"I hate to break this to you, but girls can't be knights," said Joey. "They can only be pages, heralds, or dancers. Do you believe it?"

"No, I don't believe it." Marilyn rolled her big brown eyes.

"I'm serious!" Joey replied. "Mr. Romero explained the rules in gym class this morning."

Marilyn shook her head angrily, rattling the little gold beads in her braids. "I can't believe this! What do they think—that it's really the fourteenth century? Wait till Dawn hears about this. She'll . . ."

"Wait till I hear about what?" A sweaty but smiling Dawn joined her two friends.

Marilyn repeated what Joey had just finished telling her.

"That stinks!" said Dawn. "They expect us to swish around in long skirts while the guys have all the fun?"

"That's sure what it sounds like," said Marilyn.

"Well, I'm not swishing around in anything," said Dawn angrily. "I'm going to boycott those stupid games."

"I'm with you," said Marilyn. "Now let's go. I have studying to do."

The three friends headed home. As they walked, Joey entertained the girls with zany impressions of a knight. "Unhand the princess, vile dragon!" he cried in a deep voice. He waved an invisible sword at an imaginary beast. "Back! Back, I say!" Joey pretended to charge at the dragon, then tripped himself and fell. The trio broke into laughter, but then Joey suddenly stopped. "Oh great," he said in his normal voice. "Look who it is. Here comes Sir Hot Shot."

The girls looked where Joey was pointing. Reggie Davis, quarterback of the Westwood High football team, was swaggering toward them.

"Oh man, this isn't my day," groaned Dawn.

"What's up?" asked Joey.

"Reggie's got it bad for Dawn," explained Marilyn, "and she can't stand him."

"But all the girls think he's soooooo cute," said Joey, doing a bad imitation of a girl's voice.

"Yeah, but his attitude is pretty ugly," said Dawn. "Just because he's a star quarterback, he thinks he's better than everyone else. Besides, he's a sore loser."

"When has he ever lost?" asked Joey. "Westwood's football team is practically undefeated."

"He's a loser when it comes to Dawn!" said Marilyn.

Reggie approached the group.

"Greetings, my lord," said Joey, bowing low. Even when he straightened back up, Joey looked scrawny next to Reggie. "How do you fare on this fine day?"

"What are you talking about, you joker?" asked Reggie, annoyed.

"That's jester to you, my lord," said Joey, bowing again.

"Talk sense, wimp," snarled Reggie. A

mean look clouded his handsome face.

"Give him a break. He's just practicing for Medieval Days," said Dawn. She hated to see Reggie pick on Joey. "He's going to be the jester."

"That reminds me," said Reggie. "You're a lucky girl, Dawn. I've chosen

you to be my lady at the tournament."

"What?" cried Dawn.

"It just means that you'll cheer me on and stuff," explained Reggie.

"You give me a small token like a glove or a ribbon. I wear it in my helmet, then win every event in your honor."

"I beg to remind you that you're from the rival school, my lord," said Joey. "Lady Dawn will be cheering for the noble knights of Millbrook."

"I won't be cheering for anybody, Joey. I'm boycotting the tournament," said Dawn. Then she turned angrily toward Reggie. "Listen up," she said. "I don't wear ribbons, and the only glove I have is a sweaty old workout glove. And I wouldn't even give you that! I'm not your lady or anybody else's. In fact, I'd make just as good a knight as you— probably a better one!"

"Hear! Hear!" cheered Joey.

"Can it, wimp," said Reggie abruptly. "Okay, Dawn. But you don't know what you're missing."

Dawn didn't answer. She was already striding on down the street. "Come on, guys," she called back to her friends. "We're out of here!"

CHAPTER 2

Three weeks later, a ringing sound woke Dawn. She grabbed for the phone next to her bed. "Hello?" she said sleepily.

"Awaken, lady fair."

"Joey?" Dawn moaned. She looked at the clock, which read 6:57 a.m. "It's not even seven o'clock!"

"Don't hang up," begged Joey. "I've got to talk to you."

"Make it snappy, Joey," said Dawn. "I'm going back to sleep."

"Listen," said Joey. "I need you to meet me at school."

"School?" cried Dawn. "Here's a news

flash, Joey. Today is Saturday. Now go
back to bed."

"I know it's Saturday," Joey replied.
"It's also the day of the tournament. I
have to be at school in an hour to help
set up. Then I have to change into my
jester outfit. Wait till you see my act! It
will be great preparation for drama
school someday."

"Sorry I'll miss it," said Dawn. "But

I'm skipping those stupid games, remember?"

"Dawn, please meet me," said Joey. "I have to talk to you face to face. Besides, I think you'll be interested in what I have to say."

Dawn sighed loudly. "Then say it, Joey, and stop annoying me."

"If you meet me," said Joey, "I'll let you borrow any CD I own, for as long as you want . . ." Joey had a pretty great CD collection.

"Well . . ." said Dawn.

"Please, Dawn, pleeeeeeeeease," pleaded Joey.

"Okay, okay," said Dawn, giving in. "Don't whine. I'll meet you in front of the school at eight o'clock."

"Meet me by the gym doors at 7:45," said Joey.

"Eight o'clock," repeated Dawn. "Bye." She hung up the phone.

At 8:05 Dawn was standing outside

the gym doors tapping her foot and looking at her watch. Joey was nowhere to be seen. Then she heard bells jingling. Joey burst through the double doors looking totally ridiculous. He was wearing green tights, a yellow tunic, and funny orange shoes with turned-up toes. The top part of his costume was red. It covered both his head and his shoulders, so only his face was showing. The headpiece looked like an elf's hat with points flopping down on either side of his face. There was a bell on the end of each point.

"Lady Dawn!" cried Joey.

Dawn almost fell down laughing. "Oh, Joey!" she giggled. "Don't you have an ounce of pride?"

"The lady is amused?" asked Joey.

"Very," said Dawn. "Now tell me why I'm here. And let's drop the fourteenth century talk, okay?"

"Okay," agreed Joey, speaking

normally. "Here's the deal. Derek Jackson called me last night. Man, was he sick. He got food poisoning from Speedy Burger."

"That's too bad," said Dawn. "But what's that have to do with me?"

"I'm getting to that part," said Joey. "See, Derek was supposed to be a knight for Millbrook today."

"So who'd they get to take his place?" asked Dawn.

"No one," said Joey, "because no one knows Derek is sick. I was supposed to tell Mr. Romero or one of the other teachers. But I didn't."

Dawn figured Joey was scared because he forgot to deliver Derek's message. "Look, Joey," she said, trying to help. "You can tell Mr. Romero that Derek just called you this morning. Maybe they can get a last-minute replacement. Tim Choy could do it."

"I have somebody else in mind," said

Joey mysteriously. He winked at Dawn.

"Who?" asked Dawn impatiently.

"You!" said Joey.

"Come on," said Dawn. "You know girls aren't allowed to be knights."

"Yeah, but what if no one knew?" asked Joey. "What if I snuck you into the locker room? I could stand guard while you put on Derek's knight costume. The helmet will hide your face. Come on. It would be way cool!"

"Way uncool," said Dawn. "What if I got caught?"

"You won't," argued Joey. "Think about it. You're tall and thin like Derek. You'll be in costume. You're just as good an athlete as he is . . ."

"Yeah," said Dawn, "but I'm a girl and he's a guy."

"No one will know," said Joey. "I guarantee it."

"Well, it would be great to beat some of those guys," said Dawn. She looked at Joey. "I can't believe I'm even considering this!"

"You can do it, Dawn!" Joey urged. "Besides, I've never seen you turn down a challenge. "

"You swear you won't tell anyone?" asked Dawn.

"I swear!" Joey replied.

"And you'll make sure no one sees me in the locker room?"

"I'll make double sure," promised

Joey, nodding his head.

"I must be out of my mind," said Dawn. "But I'll do it."

"All right!" Joey jumped up and down, ringing all his bells.

CHAPTER 3

The boys' locker room was empty. The other Millbrook knights had already changed into their gear and were out practicing on the field.

Dawn stood in the last row of lockers getting into Derek's costume. The tights were a little droopy, but Dawn just hiked them up as high as they would go. The black undershirt was fine, but the red tunic was big. Luckily, there was a belt to go with it. Dawn buckled it on and bloused the tunic over it. The tunic was decorated with the Millbrook crest. Dawn had to admit it looked pretty cool.

Next she pulled on the sturdy black

boots. Luckily, they fit. Dawn remembered how mad she always got when her little brother Roy called her "Bigfoot." She did have big feet—and for once she was glad about it.

Dawn glanced at the clock and realized she'd better hurry. It was 8:45 and the games where set to begin at nine o'clock.

She strapped on her armor knee pads and elbow pads. Then there were heavy

leather gloves to put on, and last came the helmet. With the visor down, it covered Dawn's whole face. She could see and breathe all right, but it sure was hot in there. Dawn told herself to just deal with it. That helmet wasn't coming off for anything!

Dawn walked a little stiffly toward the mirror. "I've got to get used to this armor—and fast!" she told herself.

When she saw her reflection, Dawn smiled beneath her helmet. "No one will know it's me," she thought.

Just then, Dawn heard a noise. The locker room door was opening! "Derek! Yo, Derek!" It was the voice of Hector Sanchez, one of Millbrook's knights.

"He's got to be in here somewhere. Joey Coletta said Derek was getting changed."

Dawn recognized the second voice. It was Mr. Romero! What if the gym teacher caught her? Dawn willed herself

to be calm, just as she did before running a race. She stepped away from the lockers and into the main aisle. Hector saw her.

"Derek, man, hurry up!" he said. "All the knights should be out on the field." Hector didn't suspect a thing! Mr. Romero smiled at her.

Dawn gave Hector a thumbs-up, then followed him and Mr. Romero out of the locker room.

"Today I'm going to prove to myself that I'm as good an athlete as anybody in this school—male or female!" thought Dawn.

She wasn't worried anymore. This was going to be fun.

CHAPTER
4

Joey the Jester caught up with Dawn as she walked toward the football field.

"Lookin' good, Sir Derek," he said.

"Thanks, Joey," said Dawn. "And thanks a lot for looking out for me, you creep. It's a good thing I had my helmet on when Hector came into the locker room!"

"Sorry about that," Joey said, "but I was setting things up for you. I told the guys that you, or Derek, that is, have laryngitis. Pretty smart, huh? I said you lost your voice. If you really have to say something, just whisper. Can you whisper in a deep voice?"

"How's this?" whispered Dawn gruffly.

"Great!" said Joey. "The helmet really muffles your voice."

"Good," said Dawn. "Hey, do you think you can slip away at some point and call Marilyn? Let her know what's going on and ask her to come down." Dawn knew she'd feel better if her friend was in the stands rooting for her.

"No sweat," said Joey. "Now you

better get over to the red tent."

Dawn hardly recognized Millbrook High's football field. The bleachers were decorated with streamers and pennants, red for Millbrook and green for Westwood. There was a red tent at one end of the field and a green tent at the other end. The knights were supposed to approach the field from their tents when the games began.

In the red tent, the Millbrook knights were complaining.

"Man, these tights itch," grumbled Eric Wilkes.

"They're called hose," said Manny Fletcher.

"Whatever you call 'em, they're a drag," said Eric.

Dawn forced herself not to laugh.

"How do you think girls stand it?" Eric continued. But Eric's questions were interrupted by the blare of trumpets. The red knights crowded

towards the opening of the tent. They
all wanted to see what was happening
on the field.

The opening ceremonies were
starting. Lawana Brown, dressed as a
herald, welcomed the challengers from

Westwood High. Then the medieval procession began.

First came the other heralds, girls and guys wearing their team's colors. Then came musicians, followed by dancers in brightly colored dresses. Next came acrobats, who flipped and cartwheeled their way across the field. And finally there was Joey. To Dawn's surprise he was juggling colored balls. Dawn had known him since they were in third

grade, and she'd never seen him juggle.

After the procession Mr. Franklin, a popular social studies teacher at Millbrook, took the microphone. He was decked out in a white and gold robe and a crown. Mr. Franklin was playing the part of the king.

"His Highness" began with a few words about tournaments during medieval times. He explained that they started as mock battles to train knights and horses for war. "Today's tournament," he said, "will be a show of athletic ability. Young men from Millbrook and Westwood will demonstrate some of the skills that real knights once needed. We hope you enjoy their demonstrations of skill and bravery."

The crowd's cheers almost drowned out another blare of trumpets. Ben Bradley in his herald's costume called to the knights. "Come forth, knights! Come forth!" The red and green knights emerged from their tents at opposite ends of the football field. Dawn jogged to the center of the field with her teammates. "This is it," she thought excitedly.

Earlier in the tent, the knights had been shown a schedule for the games. "Derek" was the red team's fourth challenger.

Joey had briefed Dawn on the obstacle course back in the locker room. It was worth up to fifteen points. Dawn ran through Joey's words in her mind.

"First you climb a rope ladder with a pool of water underneath it," he'd said. "If you make it across, that's three points. Then you swing hand-over-hand across some monkey bars for another three points. For the last part of the race, you run past a row of dummy knights that are holding wooden swords. I made one myself in

woodshop, by the way. Try to knock each sword to the ground with your sword. The swords are worth one point apiece. The king will be seated on his throne at the finish line. The race is over when the first knight falls to his, or her, knees before the king. The fastest knight gets five more points. And to make it really tough, you've got to do it all in armor!"

Dawn's thoughts were interrupted by the clanging of a bell. The race had begun!

Hector Sanchez took off against a green knight from Westwood. Halfway across the ladder he lost his footing, and splash! Hector jumped up and gave the rest of the race his best shot, but Westwood had the lead, thirteen to six.

As Hector rejoined his teammates one of the green knights called, "Hey Sanchez, nice day for a swim!" Dawn recognized the voice as Reggie Davis's.

Millbrook's next two knights had better luck than Hector. Westwood was still in the lead, but not by as much.

"Hey, Derek, you're up!" said Manny Fletcher. "I know you're not feeling well. Just do your best, man."

"Yeah, clobber that quarterback," said Eric Wilkes.

Dawn couldn't believe it. She was up against Reggie!

"Good luck," said Mike Evans,

slapping Dawn on the back.

"You'll need more than luck to beat me," said Reggie, stepping up to the starting line.

Fortunately, Dawn didn't have time to answer. The starting bell went off, and she was on her way.

Dawn was a little slow on the rope ladder, but she caught up with Reggie on the monkey bars.

Then she raced to grab her sword from the waiting page. It was heavier than it looked. She swung with all her might at the first wooden sword. It fell to the ground. So did the next two. No one had managed yet to knock down all four swords. When she came to the last one, Dawn slowed down a bit. She didn't want to miss her mark. Whoosh! She swung and the wooden sword fell! She dropped her own sword, ran forward and slid to her knees before the king. Reggie slid down next to her a few

seconds later.

Looking over her shoulder, Dawn saw that he'd missed one sword. She'd done it! She'd earned the whole fifteen points and beaten Reggie Davis!

CHAPTER 5

The next event was a foot race, and Dawn beat her opponent easily. The only person faster than she was Reggie, who topped Dawn's score by two points.

An official read the combined scores for the first two events. Millbrook was in the lead and "Derek," really Dawn— was the school's top knight. Reggie was top knight for Westwood.

The knights got a short break while the dancers performed for the crowd. Dawn was heading back to the red tent when she spied Marilyn in the first row of seats. Dawn approached her friend.

"Hey, you were great in the obstacle

course!" laughed Marilyn.

"Thanks, Marilyn," whispered Dawn hoarsely.

"Oh yeah,"said Marilyn grinning. "You have laryngitis, right *Derek*?"

Dawn just nodded as Joey approached.

"Hurry up, Derek," he said. "The archery contest is about to start."

Dawn waved to Marilyn and headed

back to the field. For the archery contest, the knights would use longbows. These were like ordinary bows, only longer, as the name implied. Real knights had used long bows during medieval times.

Millbrook still had the lead when it became Dawn's turn to shoot. She was up against Reggie again, since they were each the top knight on their teams.

Dawn was a little nervous about the longbow. Unlike the other knights, she'd never had a chance to practice with it. Then she reminded herself of the summer she'd spent as a camp counselor-in-training. She'd been a pretty good archer then. "You can do it," Dawn told herself.

Dawn and Reggie were each given three arrows.

Reggie shot first. His first arrow hit near the edge of the target. Dawn heard him curse as he tried again. The next two arrows landed close to the bullseye.

Reggie raised his visor. "Beat that, Derek," he said with a nasty smirk.

Dawn stepped up to the mark and fired her first arrow. "Not bad," she thought when it hit. She did even better

with her next two arrows. When the scores were given, Dawn had beaten Reggie by a point!

Dawn was feeling great. She high-fived her teammates and did a little victory dance. Then she heard Joey's voice near her ear.

"Chill out, Sir Happy Feet," he said. "We've got to talk."

Joey led Dawn away from the other knights. "Listen," he said. "There's trouble."

"What do you mean?" asked Dawn. "I'm doing great!"

"Yeah, but Reggie is suspicious," said Joey. "I heard him talking to his teammate, Tony Diaz."

"What did he say?" Dawn asked nervously.

"He noticed you shot that longbow with your right hand," said Joe. "Derek is a lefty! Reggie has played baseball against him enough times to know. He

also thinks it's weird that you won't raise your visor."

"Oh, no," moaned Dawn. "What do I do now?"

"Well, I think I covered the visor situation," said Jocy. "I told him you've sworn to your lady to wear it down at all times. Davis saw you talking to Marilyn, so I think he bought it."

"What about the hand thing?" asked Dawn.

"The sword fight is the last event," said Joey. "Do you think you can handle it, lefty?"

"I don't know," said Dawn with uncertainty. "But I've got to try."

CHAPTER 6

The red knights kept congratulating Dawn, telling her how great she was doing. But Dawn was so nervous, she could hardly stand still. The sword fights had begun, but Dawn didn't care how her team was doing. She just wanted to get through this last event without blowing her cover. Finally she heard Derek's name called.

Dawn met Reggie in the middle of the field. She held her sword in her left hand and her shield in her right. She took a few deep breaths, trying to steady her nerves. Then Reggie lifted his visor and spoke.

"You know, Derek," he said, "I could have sworn you were taller than I am."

Dawn gulped. She was clearly a couple of inches shorter than Reggie.

Reggie dropped his visor and shrugged. "Guess I was wrong. Oh well, may the best man win!"

And the sword fight began. Dawn was able to fend off Reggie's blows with the shield in her good hand. But the sword in her left hand was practically useless. Before long, disaster struck.

Reggie seemed to sense that Dawn's left hand was getting tired. He swung at her sword as hard as he could, and sent it clattering to the ground.

"It's over," thought Dawn. But she was wrong. Reggie rushed toward her. She thought he was going to make a snide remark about beating her. Instead he reached up and snatched off her helmet!

"Just as I thought!" Reggie cried.

There were a few seconds of silence in

the crowd. Then everyone began talking at once. Dawn stood frozen there, feeling like a loser and a fool. When she felt hot tears springing to her eyes, she bolted. She could hear people calling her name, but she kept running. Millbrook's best knight never stopped until she got home.

Hours later, Dawn's phone began to ring. She tried to ignore it, but finally picked it up on the thirty-fourth ring.

"Hey! What's up?" asked Joey cheerfully.

"Joey, I'm in no mood for chit chat," said Dawn.

"Okay, okay," he said. "Listen, you left so fast, you never heard the good news. Millbrook won the tournament thanks to you!"

"You're kidding!" said Dawn. "I thought they'd disqualify the whole team after my stupid stunt, or our stupid stunt, I should say."

"Dawn, you're overreacting," Joey replied. "Everybody thought you were awesome today. Mr. Romcro said he wishes he could draft you for the football team!"

"Stop trying to make me feel better," said Dawn. "I blew it."

"Come on," said Joey. "Everything's

cool. You'll see for yourself at the banquet tonight."

"What are you talking about?" asked Dawn.

"Don't tell me you forgot," said Joey. "There's a big bash tonight for the knights and everyone else who participated. Marilyn and I are calling from the school right now. We have to help decorate the cafeteria."

"Enjoy yourselves," said Dawn, ready

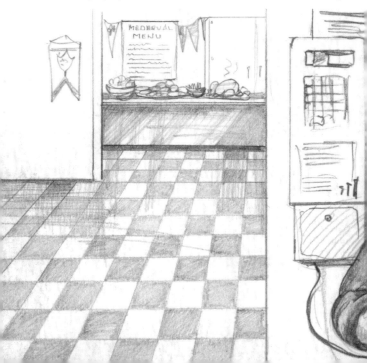

to hang up on her friend.

"You'll be there, won't you?" asked Joey.

"Joey, I don't even know if I'll be at school on Monday," answered Dawn. "How can I show my face after what happened today?"

"Wait," said Joey. There was a pause, then Marilyn got on the line.

"Dawn, I know you're embarrassed," she said, "but get over it! You should be

proud of yourself! Those games were unfair, and you were the only person brave enough to take a stand. You're a hero! You have to come tonight."

"I don't know," said Dawn.

Joe grabbed the phone. "Be there at six o'clock. We'll save you a seat." The line went dead.

At 6:15 Dawn stood outside the front door of Millbrook High. She didn't really want to be there. But she'd decided she might as well face everybody now and get it over with. She took a deep breath and went inside.

The school cafeteria was decorated to look like a medieval banquet hall. Banners and shields hung everywhere. Everyone was dressed in medieval costume. Dawn felt out of place in her jeans and T-shirt.

"Lady Dawn!" Joey the Jester met her at the door. "You're fashionably late. Come on inside and sit down."

Dawn headed for a seat next to Marilyn. On her way to the table, people called out to her.

"All right, Dawn!"

"Way to go!"

Eric Wilkes approached her. "We

couldn't have done it without you," he said. He took Dawn's arm and steered her towards the red knights' table. To her surprise, the knights began to cheer. As Dawn took her seat, the knights raised goblets of grape soda. "To our

noblest knight!" cried Eric. Everyone cheered again even louder.

Dawn couldn't believe it. She really was a hero! But just as she was beginning to enjoy herself, Dawn felt a tap on her shoulder. She looked up, and there stood Reggie Davis.

"Uh, Dawn," he began uncertainly, "I just want to say you were really good today. I don't agree with what you did, but you made your point. You, uh . . . you deserved to win." Reggie turned and quickly walked away.

Dawn was amazed. Reggie had actually admitted that she was a good knight!

There was one more surprise in store for Dawn. After dinner Mr. Franklin, the king, rose to make a proclamation.

"Thanks to today's rather surprising turn of events," he said, "the officials have made a decision. Equality will reign at next year's tournament! Girls

will be allowed to participat
knights!"

Joe the Joker raised his glass. "T
'Dawn' of a new day!" he cried.
whole crowd cheered.